A Horse to Love
An Enchanted Stables Story

By Melissa Lagonegro

Illustrated by the Disney Storybook Artists

A Random House PICTUREBACK® Bo

Random House 🏠 New Yor'

Copyright © 2007 Disney Enterprises, Inc. All r'
Published in the United States by Random House Children's Boo' c., New York,
and in Canada by Random House of Canada Limited, Toronto, in conjunction with Disney Enterprises, Inc.
Pictureback, Random House, and the Random House colophon are registered trademarks of Random House, Inc.
Library of Congress Control Number: 2007926615
ISBN: 978-0-7364-2504-9
www.randomhouse.com/kids/disney
MANUFACTURED IN CHINA   10 9 8 7   First Edition

Do you like horses? A princess certainly does—and she knows how to take extra-special care of them. Cinderella visits the horses in the palace stables every day. She especially loves spending time with Frou. Frou has been Cinderella's faithful friend since before she became a princess.

© Disney

A princess always wants her horses to be comfortable and feel at home. Belle fills the stable with flowers, blankets, and pillows—everything the horses love!

A princess feeds her horse only healthy food.
Snow White knows that apples are Astor's favorite
afternoon snack.

Belle's horses love carrots. Sometimes they can eat an entire basketful!

A princess and her horse always work together to get a job done. Snow White and Astor ride into the forest to find the Prince's lost hat.

The hat is stuck on a branch!
Astor jumps into the air while
Snow White reaches up high.

A princess enjoys taking long rides with her horse. Belle and Phillipe journey deep into the forest—where they meet a family of wild horses!

A princess likes to ride her horse in style.
Cinderella's fairy godmother makes Cinderella
and Frou sparkle and shine. Frou even gets to
wear glass horseshoes!

Snow White always places a flower in Astor's bridle before he heads off on a ride.

Cinderella and Frou like to compete in horse shows. Cinderella is very proud of her hardworking companion.